A NOTE TO PARENTS AND CAREGIVERS

Diabetes can be a frightening and confusing disease, especially for children. Not only is the disease difficult to understand, but the process of measuring blood sugar and injecting insulin can also be scary for young children as they first learn to treat their diabetes. In addition, children with diabetes can feel isolated and unable to do the things that other kids do.

As a practicing physician for thirty years and the founder of numerous health care facilities, I have learned that children have a natural curiosity and a resilience that often surprises adults. Children want and need clear explanations and straight answers to gain a sense of control over their own lives. Many parents struggle with telling their children about diabetes. Often, parents don't know how to explain the disease simply and succinctly. Sometimes, parents and caregivers provide different explanations that can cause a young child to worry. By reading this book along with a child in a medical facility, in a school, or in the home, parents and caregivers can present a standard message about diabetes that is both educational and reassuring.

All of us want to give diabetic children the knowledge, confidence, and strength they need to live happy, healthy, and normal lives. I hope that this story of superhero Katie Kate and the Worry Wombat will allow you and your child to create and maintain a positive, joyful, and open attitude about diabetes.

—M. Maitland DeLand, M.D.

Dedicated to my darling son Andrew and his
courageous and valiant effort with diabetes. —M.D.

Published by Greenleaf Book Group Press
Austin, Texas
www.gbgpress.com

Distributed by Greenleaf Book Group LLC

For ordering information or special discounts for bulk purchases, please contact
Greenleaf Book Group LLC at PO Box 91869, Austin, TX 78709, 512.891.6100.

Design and composition by Greenleaf Book Group LLC
Cover design by Greenleaf Book Group LLC
Illustrations by Jennifer Zivoin

Publisher's Cataloging-In-Publication Data (Prepared by The Donohue Group, Inc.)

DeLand, M. Maitland.
The Great Katie Kate. Discusses diabetes / M. Maitland
DeLand ; with illustrations by Jennifer Zivoin. -- 1st ed.
: col. ill. ; cm.

Summary: A superhero figure, magical Katie Kate, explains diabetes to kids in order
to increase their understanding and lessen their worries about the disease.
Interest age level: 005-010.
ISBN: 978-1-60832-039-4
1. Diabetes in children--Treatment--Juvenile fiction. 2. Diabetes--Patients--Juvenile
fiction. 3. Children--Preparation for medical care--Juvenile fiction. 4. Superheroes--
Juvenile fiction. 5. Diabetes--Patients--Fiction. 6. Medical care--Fiction. 7. Superheroes--
Fiction. I. Zivoin, Jennifer. II. Title. III. Title: Great Katie Kate discusses diabetes

PZ7.D37314 Gr 2010a
[E]   2010924700

Part of the Tree Neutral™ program, which offsets the number of trees consumed in
the production and printing of this book by taking proactive steps, such as planting
trees in direct proportion to the number of trees used: www.treeneutral.com.

Manufactured by Imago on acid-free paper
Manufactured in Singapore, April 2010
Batch No. 1

10 11 12 13 14   10 9 8 7 6 5 4 3 2 1

First Edition

THE Great Katie Kate

DISCUSSES DIABETES

M. Maitland DeLand, M.D.

with illustrations by Jennifer Zivoin

GREENLEAF
BOOK GROUP PRESS

When Andrew arrived at the carnival, he told his mom he wanted to go on every ride. But after the Tilt-A-Whirl, Andrew began to feel funny.

"I don't want to go on any more rides," he said. "I feel sick. I'm so thirsty." Andrew asked his dad to take him to the bathroom again and again.

"My legs feel like rubber, Daddy. And I'm so tired." Andrew sat down on a bench with his parents. He leaned against his dad and closed his eyes . . .

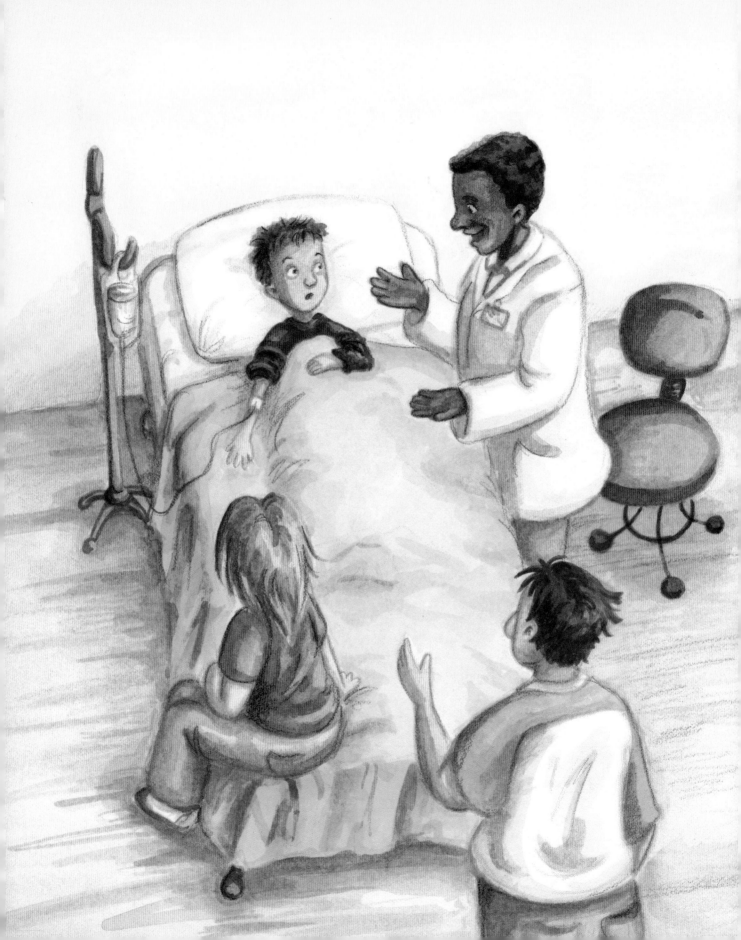

Andrew woke up on a strange bed in a strange place.

"Where am I?" Andrew asked. "What's going on?"

A man in a white coat came to his side. "I'm Dr. Caruthers," he said. "You fainted at the carnival and now you are in the hospital."

"Why did I faint?" Andrew asked.

"We think you might have something wrong with the way your body uses the sugar you eat, a condition called diabetes," Dr. Caruthers said. "We are going to take some tests. If you have diabetes, we can help you feel a whole lot better."

"Diabetes?" Andrew whispered. "What does that mean? What's going to happen to me?"

"Don't worry," Dr. Caruthers said. "I have a friend who can help."

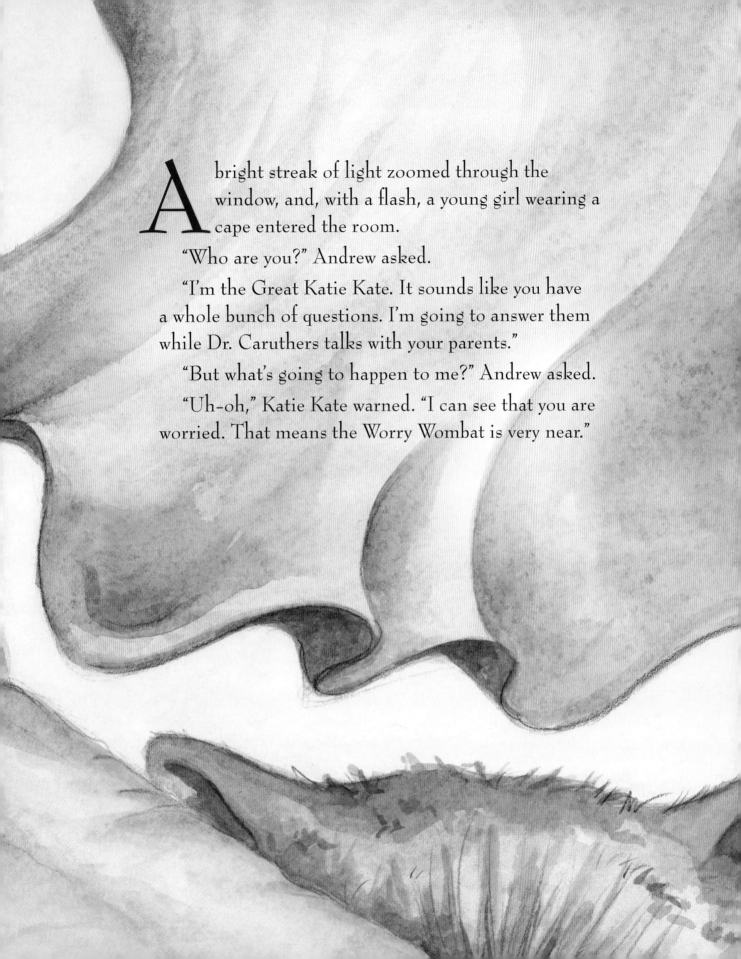

A bright streak of light zoomed through the window, and, with a flash, a young girl wearing a cape entered the room.

"Who are you?" Andrew asked.

"I'm the Great Katie Kate. It sounds like you have a whole bunch of questions. I'm going to answer them while Dr. Caruthers talks with your parents."

"But what's going to happen to me?" Andrew asked.

"Uh-oh," Katie Kate warned. "I can see that you are worried. That means the Worry Wombat is very near."

"The Worry Wombat?" asked Andrew. Just then he heard a rustling in the corner. He turned and saw a large, furry critter that looked sad and worried.

"The Worry Wombat is my name," it said with a sniffle, "and causing worries is my game."

"I don't think I like the Worry Wombat," Andrew said.

"Don't be afraid of the Worry Wombat," Katie Kate said. "All you have to do is ask questions about diabetes and smile whenever you can. Then the Worry Wombat will shrink and disappear."

Andrew worked up the courage to ask, "What is this tube doing in my arm?"

Katie Kate smiled, "Very good question, Andrew."

"This tube is giving you the fluids you need to rehydrate and stop feeling tired," Katie Kate explained.

"You're right," Andrew said. "I don't feel tired anymore."

"Good," Katie Kate said. "Keep asking questions, Andrew, and you'll feel even better."

"Dr. Caruthers said I might have diabetes," Andrew said. "What's that?"

Katie Kate smiled. "In just a minute the nurse will take the tube out of your arm, Andrew, and then I'll explain all about diabetes."

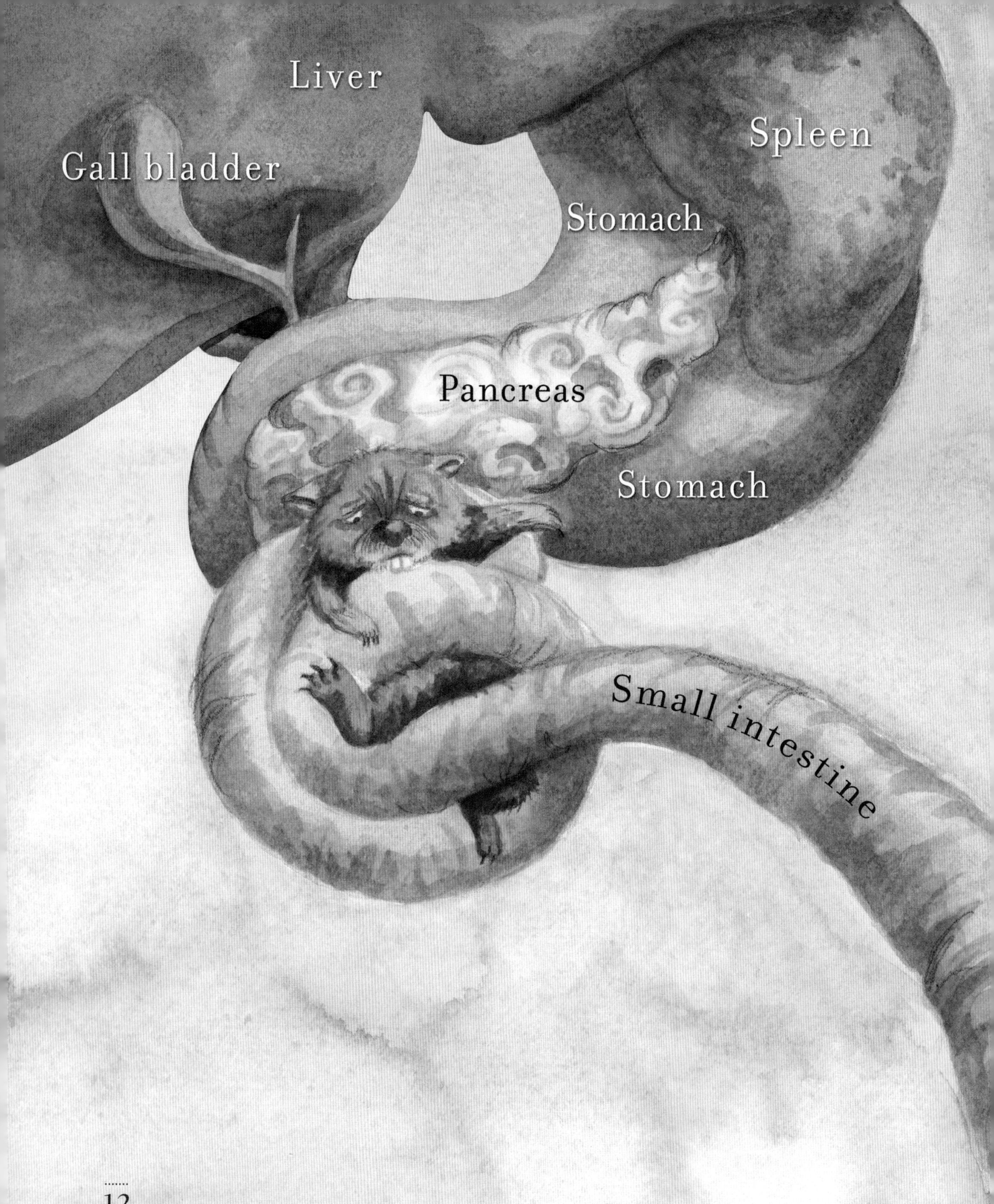

Liver

Spleen

Gall bladder

Stomach

Pancreas

Stomach

Small intestine

"Where are we?" Andrew said, looking at the strange shapes around him.

"We are inside a human body, Andrew. This is what you look like on the inside."

"What are all these big blobby things?"

"They are organs. Over there is the stomach. It digests the food that you eat. You have many organs, and each does something different. Do you see that organ over there?"

Andrew nodded.

"That is the pancreas. The pancreas makes something called insulin. You get diabetes when your pancreas stops making insulin."

"What is in-soo-lin?"

"Wow, another good question," Katie Kate said. "Look at the Worry Wombat: he's shrinking."

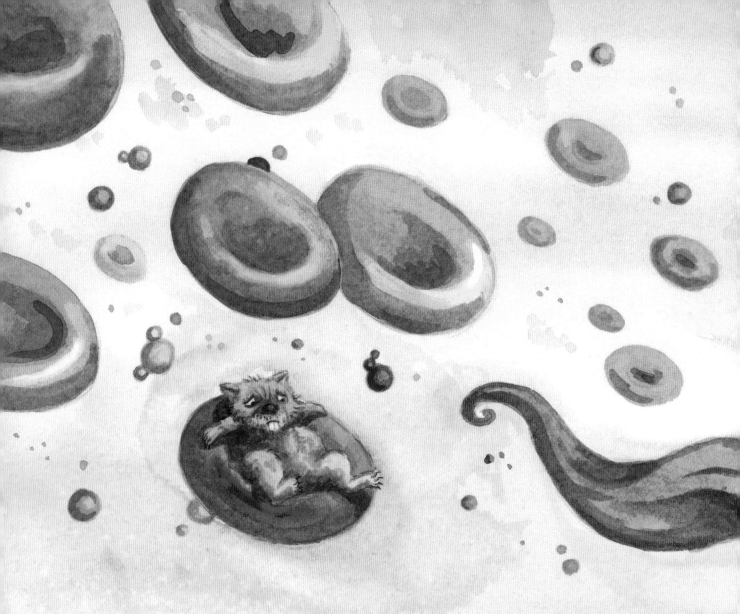

"Here we are in a blood vessel," Katie Kate said. "Do you see those blue molecules floating around?"

Andrew nodded.

"Those are glucose molecules, or sugar. When you eat food, your body breaks the food down into glucose and other molecules, and they travel into your blood. Do you see the yellow molecules?"

"Yes."

"They are insulin. When you eat and glucose enters your blood, your pancreas makes insulin. The insulin joins the glucose to make energy, which are the go-go green molecules."

"But why was I so tired?" Andrew asked. "And why did my head feel fuzzy?"

"Your pancreas was not making insulin, so your body could not make energy from the glucose in your bloodstream."

"So I felt tired because I didn't have enough insulin?"

"That's right!"

"If I have diabetes, will I ever have enough energy?"

"You'll have just as much energy as everyone else. See those kids over there in the playground?"

"Yes."

"They have diabetes."

"But they're running around and playing. They have lots of energy."

"And you'll have lots of energy, too, even if you have diabetes. Pretty soon, you'll be able to play as much as you want. All you have to do is maintain a normal blood sugar level."

"What is a blood sugar level?"

"Let's go ask my friends."

"Hi, Katie Kate," the girl said. "Who's your friend?"

"Hello, Maria. Hello, Howard," said Katie Kate. "Meet Andrew. He may have diabetes just like you."

"Hi, Andrew," they said together.

"You look a little bit worried," said Maria. "Can we help?"

"Um . . . what is a blood sugar level?" Andrew asked, feeling a little shy.

"Your blood sugar level is the amount of glucose or sugar in your blood," Maria said.

"When your pancreas is working, it knows your blood sugar level and produces just the right amount of insulin to help turn that sugar into energy," Howard explained.

"Because my pancreas doesn't work," Maria said, "I need to check my blood sugar level myself."

"How do you do that?" Andrew asked.

"I have to give myself a finger stick—just a prick of my finger—with a little needle called a lancet," Maria said. "Watch Howard."

"First, I insert the glucose meter strip into my meter. Then I poke my finger with the lancet and a tiny drop of blood comes out. Then I take the tiny drop of blood and put it on the glucose meter strip, and the meter shows me my blood sugar level."

"I don't like the finger stick and blood parts," Andrew said, feeling frightened.

"It doesn't hurt much at all," Maria said. "Everyone with diabetes does it."

"How will I know when I need a finger stick?" Andrew asked.

"Well, when my blood sugar level isn't normal," Howard said,

"I feel tired, cranky, weak, confused, or shaky. When I feel like that, I give myself a finger stick right away. And I always check my blood sugar before and after meals and before I go to sleep. Right now my blood sugar is too low."

"What do you have to do now?" Andrew asked.

"When my blood sugar is too low," Maria said, "I need to eat or drink something that my body can turn into glucose, like peanut butter crackers or fruit juice."

"That sounds like fun," Andrew said. "And what do you do if your blood sugar is too high?"

"When my blood sugar is too high, I need insulin."

"That's why you were so thirsty and fainted at the carnival, Andrew," Katie Kate explained. "You needed insulin."

"How do you get insulin in your body?" Andrew asked.

Maria held up a syringe. "I take insulin by giving myself a shot, just like the doctor gives you sometimes."

"Does it hurt?"

"It just feels like being pricked with a needle," Maria said with a shrug.

"And I have a pump right here in my stomach that gives me insulin," Howard said.

Andrew looked puzzled. "Like a bicycle pump?"

"No, it's a lot smaller. I can hardly even feel it. I load the pump with insulin, and it helps me keep just the right amount of insulin in my body."

"Can I eat most anything I want?" Andrew asked.

"Yes. All you have to do is use this chart before you eat anything," Katie Kate said.

"On one side is the food you want to eat, in the middle is the number of carbohydrates that food has, and on the other side is how much insulin it takes to turn it into energy."

Andrew was confused. "What's a carbohydrate?"

"It's another name for the sugar in your food."

"This says 1 banana = 15 carbs = 1 unit of insulin." Andrew said.

"Right," Maria replied. "So if I eat one banana, I need one unit of insulin to change the 15 carbs in the food into energy."

ndrew shook his head. "This all sounds so complicated. Blood sugar levels, finger sticks, carbs, insulin . . ."

Katie Kate stood up straight. "It is complicated, Andrew, but you just have to remember three steps: First, do the finger stick to see if your blood sugar is low or high. Next, if your blood sugar is too low, eat something, and if your blood sugar is too high, give yourself insulin. Finally, give yourself insulin for any foods you eat, using the chart we showed you. If you do all that, you'll feel great and have lots of energy."

"Hey, come on and play basketball with us, Andrew," Maria said.

"Maybe later, Maria," Katie Kate suggested. "Right now I've got something I want to give Andrew."

"Here it is, Andrew," Katie Kate beamed. "Your own diabetes kit."

"It looks cool," Andrew said. "But what's in it?"

"Your kit has a lancet for your finger stick, a meter, strips, syringe, insulin, and some food. It's important that you always keep it with you."

"Having my own kit sounds great," Andrew said with a big smile. "I'm not worried about having diabetes anymore, because now I know how to keep my blood sugar level normal so that I can do anything I want, just like my new friends."

"Way to go, Andrew," Katie Kate cheered. "And look, the Worry Wombat has disappeared!"

The Great Katie Kate zoomed out of the window, just as Dr. Caruthers and Andrew's parents walked in.

"Mommy! Daddy!" Andrew shouted. "The Great Katie Kate came to help me and I asked a lot of questions and the Worry Wombat disappeared."

30

"Katie Kate? The Worry Wombat?"
Andrew's dad asked. "What are you
talking about, son?"

"I know just what he's talking about,"
Dr. Caruthers said, and he patted
Andrew's shoulder. "You're a very brave
boy, Andrew. And now you know that
diabetes is something you can control.
You'll soon be able to run and play and
do everything your friends do."

"Can we go back to the carnival, Mommy?" Andrew asked.

"Sure we can," his mom said. "And if you start feeling bad . . ."

"I'll know just what to do," Andrew said with a huge smile. "I'm not worried about having diabetes anymore."

The End.